To all those who look for love and help it grow.

PHILOMEL BOOKS

An imprint of Penguin Random House LLC, New York

First published in the United States of America by Philomel,
an imprint of Penguin Random House LLC, 2021.

Copyright © 2021 by Mike Malbrough.

Philomel Books is a registered trademark of Penguin Random House LLC.

Visit us online at penguinrandomhouse.com

Library of Congress Cataloging-in-Publication Data is available.

Manufactured in China

ISBN 9780593203521

1 3 5 7 9 10 8 6 4 2

Edited by Cheryl Eissing.

Design by Monique Sterling.

Text set in P22 Mayflower.

Artwork created using watercolor and gouache.

LOVE IS HERE

BY

MIKE MALBROUGH

PHILOMEL

Shh.

Listen.

Can you hear it?

RUMBLE.

Hidden in the storm clouds.

Stored up and waiting.

Small drops drum on
your coat, wrist, and palm.

They beat louder and louder.

It's time for a celebration.

Love is here.

Everything is quiet now. Is love still here?

YES!

The dry earth crackles and drinks the rainwater.

Love wriggles down, feeding green things that
sprout with the softest . . .

POP!

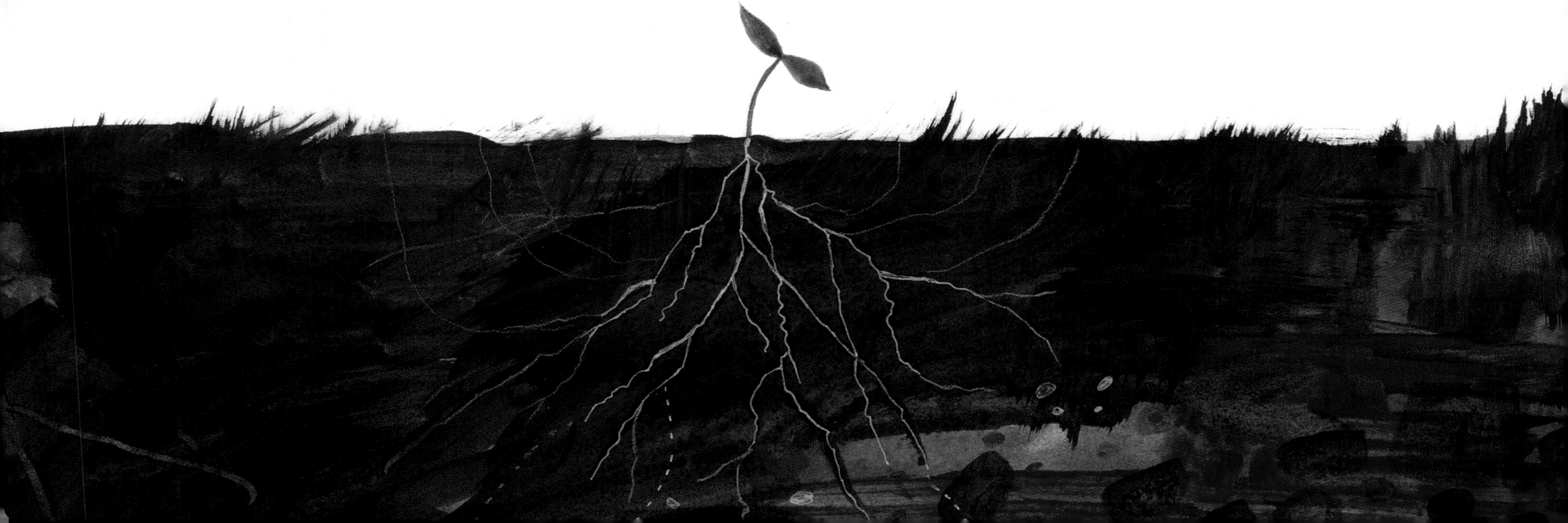

Take a deep breath.
What smells so sweet?

It's small but beautiful.
And, oh, how it moves!
Love is reaching out, growing.

Where's it going in such a hurry?

Dancing and bending in the breeze,
love carries all kinds of things.

Balloons, pollen, seeds, and wings.

Where is love taking them?

Love lands, sending ripples out across the water as shining fish race the current.

The moon is bright and full.

Look beneath the surface.

Love is there, too.

How far down does it go?

Love is calling from the deep.

Soft, low, and swelling with mystery.

Can love be more amazing than this?

And even when you are alone, love is here.
It presses back against the vast darkness.

Wings flutter onto
your hands and rest.

Love is yours.

Hold it gently.

Can you feel it tugging?

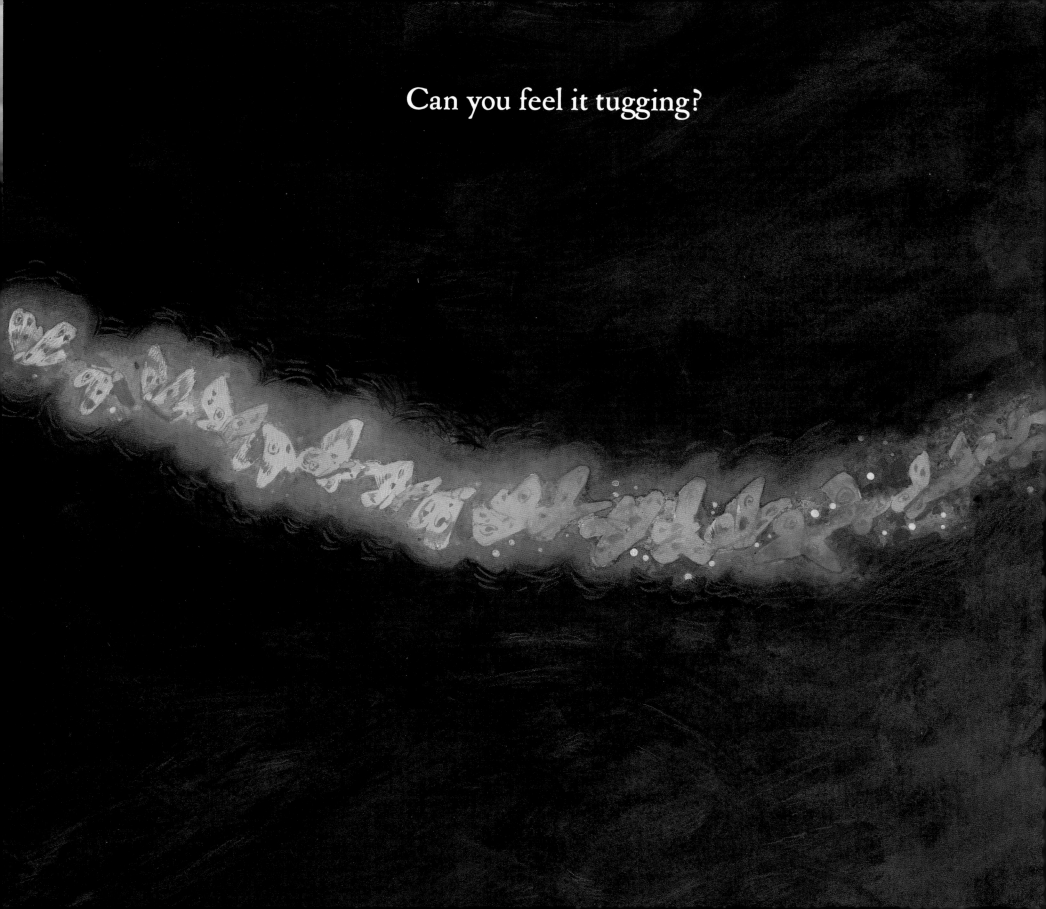

Love lifts you up, higher and higher,
into the bright fullness.

Is love here too? Yes.

You can see it in the earth . . .

and all of its neighbors.

Love is here.

Bright, free, and closer than you think.

Ready to be shared.